THE DAY MY FAMILY DISAPPEARED

Jo Simmons

Illustrated by
Lee Cosgrove

Barrington Stoke

*For Helen, with deep thanks for all
your hard work and support*

First published in 2022 in Great Britain by
Barrington Stoke Ltd
18 Walker Street, Edinburgh, EH3 7LP

www.barringtonstoke.co.uk

Text © 2022 Jo Simmons
Illustrations © 2022 Lee Cosgrove

A CIP catalogue record for this book is available
from the British Library upon request

ISBN: 978-1-80090-107-0

Printed by Hussar Books, Poland

THE DAY
MY
FAMILY
DISAPPEARED

CONTENTS

CHAPTER 1

Simply Bob

Bob Bunyon was sitting at the kitchen table. He had a mound of cold mashed potato in front of him, left over from last night's dinner. Bob was busy moulding the potato with his hands.

His sister India walked in.

"What's that supposed to be?" she asked, looking at the mashed potato.

"A cat," said Bob.

"It looks more like something a cat would throw up," India said. "Wow, Bob, you're not even a tiny bit creative, are you?"

"I am," said Bob. "I come up with lots of creative ways to avoid you and everyone else in this house. Yesterday, I hid in a wardrobe for three hours and no one found me."

"That's because no one noticed you were gone," India said. "You're almost invisible. I don't get how you belong in this family. We're all artists and performers, and you're just …"

"Normal," Bob muttered.

He left his potato sculpture and went to sit in the garden, as far away from the noisy, busy house as he could get. India was right. Bob's parents and four siblings were all artists and performers – or "show-offs", as Bob liked to put it.

His dad made banjos and his mum was a nature poet, which meant she wrote about slugs and ferns and rain. Bob's brother River was brilliant at circus skills and his other brother, Cosmo, was a street-dancer. His sister India was an amazing baker – she once made a cake shaped like a windmill, with spinning sails. Bob's other sister, Arwen, was an opera singer.

Last and also least was Bob. He was the youngest of them all and had no obvious talents or skills (apart from making mashed potato look like cat sick). He was just a normal boy who liked TV, Hula Hoops and hanging out with his best friend, Bill. Bob didn't even have a fancy name. He was the fifth child and his mum and dad had run out of inspiration by then. That's why Bob was just … Bob.

Arwen's singing shattered the silence of the garden. Bob groaned. He hated opera. All those long screeching notes! It sounded like squirrels were pulling Arwen's hair. Then came the sound of his dad strumming a banjo. Bob covered his ears and stared angrily at the house, willing everyone inside to shut up and be normal. Why couldn't they watch a film or go to the park?

Then Cosmo came into the garden dancing and River walked out on his hands. There was India, throwing his potato sculpture in the bin.

"I wish you'd all just go away!" Bob growled.

But no one heard. Of course they didn't. They were all too busy being show-offs. Bob felt small. Maybe India was right, Bob thought. Maybe he *was* almost invisible. Did anyone care about him at all?

CHAPTER 2

Gone

When Bob woke up the next morning, he knew something was different.

The house was quiet. Silent. Still. There was no sound of opera singing or banjo strumming or cake beaters whirring.

Bob sat up in bed, bumping his head on the roof beams of his tiny attic room. He listened some more. Still nothing.

Bob opened the hatch that was his bedroom door and climbed down the ladder to the first floor of the house. He looked in all the bedrooms. No one was there. He ran downstairs, checked the living room – empty. The kitchen – deserted. The dance and circus-skills studio – nothing. The banjo workshop – completely clear. The garden – not a sausage.

"Mum? Dad?" Bob called. "Arwen? River? India? Cosmo?"

No answer. The house was empty. This was really odd. Unheard of, actually. Bob realised he'd never, ever been alone in his home. Not once in his entire life.

He let out a whoop. Just yesterday he'd wished everyone would go away – and now they had. Brilliant!

Dreams do come true, Bob thought as he opened the fridge. There was hardly any "real" food inside, just lots of India's fancy cream cakes that she never let Bob eat. Well, India wasn't here, was she? So ...

Bob sat on the kitchen floor in his pyjamas and scoffed three eclairs and a big chunk of creamy sponge. He was about as happy as

he'd ever felt. Then he set off to explore the house. As he had no real artistic skills, he didn't normally go into any of the rooms meant for performing and practising. Plus his siblings *never* let him into their bedrooms. Now was his chance.

In the banjo workshop, Bob picked up one of his dad's banjos and made up a song as he clanged the strings.

"Banjo, banjo, banjo, like a strangled dodo, or a broken yoyo, at a rubbish dog show, oh no, oh no, banjo!"

Next, Bob found River's juggling balls in the dance and circus-skills studio. He wandered into the garden, trying to juggle. But instead he chucked them over the fence by accident. Bob heard next door's dog bark with excitement and begin to chew the balls.

Up in India's room, Bob bounced on her bed and then doodled in her favourite recipe books.

He gave some cakes moustaches and drew dinosaurs climbing up others.

In Arwen's bedroom, Bob dressed up in some of the shiny necklaces and feather scarves that she wore for her opera performances. Then Bob went next door to Cosmo's room and put on his brother's coolest pair of trainers.

He checked the mirror to see if he looked good (he did), then went downstairs and fell onto the sofa.

The silence settled around Bob. He listened for a sound, any sound. The family minibus pulling up outside. A key in the door. His mum or dad calling out, "Hey, Bob, we're home." Nothing.

Bob checked the clock – 10 a.m. Where *were* they?

CHAPTER 3

Ghost Town

Bob lay on the sofa for a bit longer. A tricky thought was forming in his brain, like a mushroom growing fast. The thought was this: *What if I made my family disappear? What if my wish yesterday that they would all go away made them go away? Maybe permanently. And for ever.* (Which was the same thing, so just as worrying.)

The thought was so alarming that Bob decided he had to do something. He leapt up, tore off Arwen's feather scarf and necklace and threw on some clothes. Then he burped a greasy cake burp and raced out of the front door, determined to find his family.

The road outside was quiet, which was normal. But once Bob got near to the centre of town, he realised *everywhere* was quiet. It was a Saturday, it should have been buzzing, but there were no cars on the roads or people shopping. No kids in the playground or teenagers by the chip shop. No flower seller selling flowers. No older people playing bingo and eating crumpets at the Older People's Bingo and Crumpet Club.

Bob peered into silent shops that were all locked up. He climbed the fountain in the square – now turned off – but couldn't see anyone from high up. He explored the deserted play area in the park, but he got the creeps when he saw the swings hanging limply and heard the roundabout creaking in the breeze. Bob was starting to feel like the only survivor of a zombie invasion.

"It's not just my family who have disappeared – everyone has," Bob said to no one, as there was no one there.

He blinked hard. Had he managed to wish them all away? Was that possible? Bob didn't want to think he had that kind of power. He was a normal kid, right? Not some evil genius whose deadly mind-waves could make everyone in a town vanish overnight.

He'd better go to the police. They had to know what was going on.

Bob pushed open the heavy door to the police station and felt relief fill him like warm honey. There, at the front desk, was Sergeant Bill.

"Hello, young man. What can I do you for?" said Sergeant Bill, chuckling. "Sorry, I couldn't resist. It's a classic police joke. What can I do *for you*?"

"I can't find my family," said Bob.

"Oh dear," said Sergeant Bill. "Have you looked for them in the normal places? Down the back of the sofa, behind the fridge?"

"Yes, and they've gone," said Bob. "When I woke up this morning, the house was empty."

"Have you tried calling them?" Sergeant Bill asked.

"We don't have phones," said Bob. "My mum and dad don't believe in mobiles."

"Well, they're real," said Sergeant Bill. "I've got one right here – look!"

He thrust his phone at Bob.

"I mean, Mum and Dad don't believe in us *having* mobile phones," Bob explained. "They think we'll be on them all the time and stop being creative. Not that I am very creative, but still … What should I do?"

"You should not worry, that's what you should do," Sergeant Bill said cheerfully. "Things go missing all the time. Car keys. Socks. Umbrellas. Cats. Sausage rolls. Spanners.

Earrings. Pencils. Carrots. The list goes on. You can hunt all over the house for them and never find them. Then they just show up."

"But this is my family!" said Bob. "Six people! How can they all be gone?"

"Aliens?" said a voice from under the desk. Then a face appeared.

"Bill! I didn't know you were there," said Bob. Bill Junior was Bob's best friend, who also happened to be Sergeant Bill's son. Bill Junior liked to hang out at the police station with his dad, helping to fight crime (sometimes from under the desk).

"It could have been aliens," Bill repeated.

"Interesting thought," said his dad. "Bob, did you see any evidence of aliens? Spaceships? Lights in the sky? Slime?"

"No," said Bob. "Please can you help me find my family?"

"That might be a bit tricky," said Sergeant Bill. "It's only me and Bill Junior on duty today, see? We need to stay here. If we're wandering about looking for your family, we might miss the actual crime when it happens."

"But there's no one in town," Bob protested. "Have you been out there? It's completely empty. How can there be any crime if there aren't any people?"

"Animal crime?" suggested Bill Junior.

"Yes, son," said his dad. "Excellent police work. Animal crime. A lion escaping from the zoo, for instance."

"What zoo? There isn't a zoo in this town," Bob said.

"Do you think that will stop the lions from trying to escape wherever they are?" Sergeant Bill said sternly. "They'll head straight for our town with dark thoughts of eating people. They could be on their way right now. In fact, you should get home before they arrive, young man. If you see any lions, don't approach them. We'll handle it. That's what we're here for."

Bob sighed and left. He stopped on the steps outside the police station, unsure what to do next.

"Are you OK, Bob?" Bill Junior called behind him. "You've been doing double blinks. You do those when you're nervous."

"I'm not nervous," Bob shot back.

"Don't worry," said Bill Junior, patting Bob's arm. "I'm sure your family will be back any minute. Dad's probably right. Best to go home and wait for them. I'll let you know if we hear anything."

Bob nodded. He wasn't sure about the "go home and wait" idea. He knew that lions were not about to invade the town, but he wasn't sure that his family would suddenly return. Bob felt horribly lonely at the thought of returning to a silent, empty house, but what else could he do?

CHAPTER 4

Hunting and Hiding

Bob hurried back along the deserted streets. He began to imagine that all the town's people had not really disappeared but were hiding behind trees. He pictured them sniggering at him, ready to jump out and explain that this was all a joke and he'd fallen for it.

Bob walked faster, keeping his eyes down. As he turned onto his road, he thought he heard his family's minibus. He spun around. No. It was just a plane overhead. He rushed into his house.

"Mum? Dad?" Bob called. Silence.

He locked the front door fast. He drew the curtains too, but he wasn't sure why. Who was going to look in? No one! Unless this really was a zombie invasion and they were searching for him. Oh help! Or maybe some lions had escaped from a zoo after all and were about to stare hungrily through the window.

"Get a grip, Bob," he told himself. "You're panicking. You need to calm down."

Talking aloud helped Bob to calm his nerves.

"Right, the fact is, I have no idea where my family has gone. I could be alone for hours, maybe even overnight. My only grandparents live in Australia and it's the middle of the night there, so I'd better not ring them. I'm on my own, with only some tips I've learned from TV survival expert Lofty Gills to help me. What would Lofty do first? I know! Check supplies."

Bob rushed into the kitchen and opened the cupboards. He found two cans of baked beans and a tin of peaches. Hardly anything! He would need more than that if he was going to survive.

He grabbed the plastic bow and arrow his brothers River and Cosmo had given him last Christmas, unlocked the back door and ran into the garden. But what could Bob hunt out there? Some caterpillars? A sparrow?

Still, he hid behind a tree and waited for prey to arrive. After what felt like hours – but was in fact about three minutes – a fat pigeon landed on a branch above him. Squinting, Bob aimed at the bird and then – *WHOOSH!* – let his arrow fly.

It soared up and then bounced off a branch with a *DOINK* and plummeted down. The pigeon cocked its head and looked at the arrow, now stuck in a flowerbed, then flew off.

Bob angrily threw the bow into the bushes and stomped back inside. Hunting was hard. Really hard. No wonder most people went to the supermarket to buy food instead. *He* couldn't do that though. Bob had no money. How was he supposed to survive?

He poured himself a glass of water and sat down, but all he could hear was his own rapid breathing. Bob missed the sound of Cosmo's dance music, and his mum mumbling poetry, even Arwen's operatic wailing. He longed to see India icing a wedding cake or River rigging up his tightrope in the garden.

The empty rooms that had felt like an adventure playground to Bob this morning now felt huge and spooky. Bob couldn't stand them. He ran up the ladder to his tiny attic room, slammed the hatch down and sat on the bed, hugging his knees to his chest.

He couldn't believe they had left him. Yes, he had wished his family would go away, but not for this long. Where were they? Didn't they care? What would happen if they never came back? Would they find nothing but Bob's skeleton, still wearing Cosmo's trainers, slumped on the bed?

Bob knew then that he had to record what was happening – for the future, just in case. Like a castaway or a prisoner or someone stuck up a mountain might do. He grabbed a notebook from his desk and wrote **Bob's Abandonment Journal** in thick black letters on the cover.

Then Bob began to write.

These are the last known thoughts of Bob Bunyon, aged 10. It's August 4th and I have been alone since I woke up at 7.50 a.m. today. Totally alone.

My parents and all four brothers and sisters are gone. Yes, gone. I don't know where or why or how. They left no note. It looks like I have been abandoned!

I have tried to keep my spirits up, but they are falling. Will I ever be rescued? Is there any hope?

If I don't make it out alive, I want Mum and Dad to know that I love them (apart from today when you have let me down big time). I want River, Arwen,

India and Cosmo to know that I also love
them. Well, I like them. Well, I don't
mind them, even though they are really
annoying and show off so much.

I hereby make a confession too.
I broke the window in the front room
last week. It didn't really smash when
some ducks flew into it like I said. I was
trying to street dance, like Cosmo, and
my shoe flew off. There. Now you know.

Despite this, please remember all
that was good about me – my large
thumbs, my impression of a puffin,
and how I once made you all laugh by
snorting sweetcorn out of my nose.

Bob blinked hard. Tears were blurring his
vision. He pulled his duvet around him and
began writing again.

There is still fresh water in the taps, but I don't know how long it will last. I have only a few supplies, including baked beans, which I don't even like. I could dig up the bone that next door's dog buried yesterday. Perhaps I could make some soup from it?

The power could go out at any time, but I have found some candles and I will try to make them last. I picked off some old chewing gum from under my desk. The sight of it is cheering me up, but I'll save chewing it until later. I could be up here for hours.

Bob stared at that last sentence and was suddenly overcome with tiredness. He pulled the duvet over his head and fell into a deep sleep.

CHAPTER 5

Operation Find My Family

The sound of a vehicle woke Bob.

"A car? A car!" he squeaked. Bob tumbled
out of bed, raced downstairs and outside. The
car was already at the top of the road, turning
the corner. Bob ran after it.

"Come back! Wait!"

Bob wished he had a whistle or a flare or
something to catch the driver's attention. But

it was only him, running along in his brother's trainers, yelling and waving his arms.

Bob turned the corner of his road, panting, and saw that the car was now just a dot in the distance.

"Come back!" Bob called one last time, but the car was gone.

"Arrggghh," Bob roared, then kicked a bin and punched a bush.

This was the only human life he'd seen all day, apart from Sergeant Bill and Bill Junior, and it had got away.

Was that his last chance of rescue? His only hope?

Bob had wandered away from his road, lost in gloomy thoughts, and that was when he saw it. A poster in a shop window.

THE GREEN YON GATHERING
Rural Festival and Traditional Celebration

• Beard Weaving! • Tea-Leaf Art •
• Folk-Tune Humming •

Enjoy some ancient pastimes:

• Jump the Goat! • Spin the Cowpat! •
• Beetle Wrestling! •
• Guess the Weight of the Weasel! •

Plus rituals from the old days, including the
Ceremony of the Burning of the Rugs

Venue: Old Munty's Farm,
4–5 August

"Wait," said Bob, "4 August? That's today!"

Details from the last few weeks started popping into his mind. Arwen had been humming folk tunes, his dad had been growing his beard extra long and India had got an old rug from the loft. They had been preparing for this festival!

"That's where my family will be!" Bob cried. "I have to go there and find them!"

He raced home and went to the kitchen. Bob opened the can of peaches and spread out a map on the table. He spooned the slippery peach slices into his mouth while searching for Old Munty's Farm, where the Green Yon Gathering was taking place. It was about three miles north-west of the town. There hadn't been any buses running, and he didn't have any money for a taxi, so he'd have to walk there.

Bob studied the route. He needed to walk out of town past the retail park, into the woods, cross one field, over the stream, cross another and TA-DA! He'd be there.

"Should be all right," Bob said to himself, "but this is no stroll round the park. This is Operation Find My Family – the biggest, most important journey of my life. I must be prepared."

Bob knew all about surviving an expedition thanks to bushcraft legend Lofty Gills. He had seen all Lofty's shows. Bob's favourites were *Extreme Bog Survival*, *Cold Endurance Trek* and *Now It's Really Cold Endurance Trek*. His family used to tease him for watching Lofty's TV programmes when he could have been writing poetry or riding a unicycle, but Bob guessed the skills he learned from them would come in handy one day. Now that day had arrived.

First, Bob needed water. He filled a flask and dropped it into his backpack. Then he added a tin of baked beans, an onion and some raisins he found at the back of the cupboard.

"What else would Lofty pack?" Bob said. "Some rope!"

Unfortunately, Bob couldn't find any rope, so he had to take a ball of string instead.

A whistle might be useful, Bob thought, but he couldn't find one of those either. However, there was a red-foil party blower, left over from Arwen's birthday, so he packed that.

Then Bob found a small saucepan, because "Lofty's always cooking over an open fire", some washing-up liquid that he could also use as soap, and three teabags.

He opened the fridge – which only contained cream cakes. *Oh well*, Bob thought, and chucked a couple of them into his bag.

Finally, he grabbed two teaspoons and some paper clips that could double as fish hooks. He could fix them to the string. Perfect. Done.

"Now, I need to get changed," Bob said.

Lots of layers – that was the best thing, wasn't it? In case the weather turned suddenly. Bob began with a vest, then a T-shirt, then a sweatshirt, then a fleece. On his legs, he had shorts inside jeans inside jogging bottoms. Bob pulled Cosmo's cool trainers back on and now he finally felt ready (and also rather hot).

Just as Bob was about to leave his room, he spotted the old chewing gum and tucked it in his pocket. Then he remembered **Bob's Abandonment Journal** and quickly added a new entry.

3 p.m. These are my last recorded words before I set off on an expedition to find my family. I have packed supplies, survival gear and I am dressed correctly. Lofty Gills would be well impressed. There is no time to lose. I plan to reach the Green Yon Gathering before nightfall, all being well. Once I find my family, I expect tears of joy but also a chance to have a massive go at them for leaving me behind in the first place. How could they? But enough. No more questions. I leave now, this instant. Goodbye.
Signed – Bob Bunyon

Bob climbed down the ladder from his room. He was about to run downstairs when he thought of the lions that might be busting out of a nearby zoo and heading for town to gobble him up.

He was still pretty sure this wouldn't happen, but to be on the safe side, he rushed into the bathroom. Bob found the make-up Arwen used for her opera performances. He smeared green eyeshadow on his face as camouflage. But would the lions still smell him? Perhaps he should use some of River's body spray? Or would the scent give him away? He sprayed a bit under his arms.

Back in the kitchen, Bob swung the backpack onto his shoulders and grabbed the map. Feeling nervous but determined, he hurried out of the front door in the direction of Old Munty's Farm.

As Bob disappeared round the corner at the top of his road, a car pulled round the corner at the bottom. A police car. It was Sergeant Bill.

Had he been one minute earlier, he would have caught Bob before he left. Sergeant Bill would have told Bob that his mum had called the police station, that she had realised Bob had been accidentally left behind in the house and that she would come to pick him up that evening, after her poetry recital.

But Sergeant Bill was just a fraction too late. He knocked on the front door and got no answer, so he stuffed a note explaining what had happened into the letterbox. Then Sergeant Bill drove away, eager to get back to the police station in case any crime occurred.

CHAPTER 6

Into the Woods

Bob was soon at the retail park on the edge of town. It was deserted of course.

He tramped across the car park, feeling hot, and stopped outside a big electrical shop to take off his fleece and jogging bottoms. The massive TVs inside that normally blazed brightly were blank screens now.

Bob drank some water and ate the raisins, but nothing else – he had to ration his supplies, just in case.

Then he set off into the woods.

Bob had never walked here before. He knew which direction to follow to reach the field beyond, but the path soon ran out.

Is this right? he wondered.

He tried to remember how Lofty Gills had navigated by the sun in the episode "Utterly Out-There Desert Challenge", but it was cloudy and Bob couldn't get a clear view past the leaves above anyway.

Never mind. Keep going, he told himself.

The trees were really thick now. Bob's jeans snagged on brambles, low branches swished in his face and then … What was that? Rustling to his left. Bob stared. Nothing there.

"It's not lions," Bob told himself sternly. "Not. Lions."

He trudged on. He was getting tired and sloppy, tripping up more. Bob slipped down a bank and twisted his ankle in a rabbit hole. Then he noticed that he was back at the same fallen tree he had passed ten minutes ago. His heart thudded.

"I'm going round in circles," Bob squeaked, blinking hard. *Don't panic*, he thought. Bob wanted to run around screaming "I'm lost, I'm lost" at the top of his lungs but stopped himself. He had to stay calm.

Bob trekked on, but there was still no path, no sight of green fields past the trees. Then he spotted something in the mud. Paw marks! Big ones. Big enough to be a lion's?

Bob didn't wait to find out. He ran hard, crashing through the undergrowth, stumbling over fallen branches and gasping for breath. Sweat trickled down his face and into his eyes, streaking lines in his green camouflage and blurring his vision. Bob blinked fast, tried

to wipe it away and then … *CRASH!* He hit something solid, warm and furry.

As Bob fell to the ground, his only thought was: *This is it. I've run into the lions and now they're going to eat me.* He squeezed his eyes shut, frozen with fear. Bob heard the sound of animal panting getting nearer. He felt warm breath on his face.

Goodbye, world. Goodbye, family. Goodbye, everything, Bob thought as he waited for the end. Then ...

SLURP.

A giant tongue sloshed across Bob's face.

SLURP.

It did it again.

"Bob, is that you?"

Someone spoke. It was a voice Bob recognised.

"It's me, Mrs Remus. Remember? Your teacher at infant school. Don't mind Bear."

So Bob was being attacked by a bear, not a lion. How terrible! But why didn't Mrs Remus sound worried?

He opened one eye. There was no bear, but there was a giant dog panting above him, his big pink tongue like a slice of ham.

"He's a Leonberger – a gentle giant of a dog," said Mrs Remus, holding out a hand to Bob. "Come on, up you get. Ooh, you're shaking."

She helped Bob to a small camp under the trees and sat him by the fire.

"I love wild camping," Mrs Remus explained. "It's a hobby of mine. I'm a big fan of Lofty Gills."

"Me too," Bob said. His voice sounded weak. He was still feeling shocked after thinking a bear was attacking him.

Mrs Remus passed him a cheese sandwich.

"Thank you," he said, gobbling down mouthfuls. "I've only eaten cream cakes and peaches and raisins today. I've been alone. I wished my family would disappear and they did. I thought it was my fault, but now I think they're at a festival, so I'm going to find them. I got a bit lost, that's all."

"It's very easy to get lost in these woods," said Mrs Remus. "I rely on Bear as a guide. It's also very hard to find people at festivals. There could be thousands there. The whole town has gone."

Bob gulped. He had been so focused on making it to the festival, he hadn't thought about how he'd actually find his family, among crowds of people, once he got there.

"Perhaps I should come with you," Mrs Remus added. "I can help you find them."

Bob said nothing. It was tempting to let Mrs Remus help, but he had planned Operation Find My Family on his own. It was his chance to prove he wasn't just the uncreative odd one out, who made potato sculptures of cat sick and got ignored by everyone.

"Wait here while I go and wash the plates in the stream," Mrs Remus said. "Then we'll pack up the camp and head off."

Bob watched her go and then leapt up and ran over to Bear.

"Mrs Remus says you guide her around these woods," he said to the dog. "Can you lead me to the field, boy? The one on the other side? Can you?"

Bear stood up, shook himself and walked off.

"I'll take that as a yes," Bob said. He grabbed his backpack and dashed after the dog.

CHAPTER 7

Animal Attack!

Bear plodded through the trees and Bob followed along behind. Bob felt bad about leaving Mrs Remus without saying goodbye and borrowing her dog too. But soon he just felt tired, so he heaved himself onto the dog's broad back. Bob dropped his arms around Bear's powerful shoulders, buried his face in the dense, soft fur of his neck and dozed. Until Bear stopped and shook himself, sending Bob tumbling to the ground.

Bob sat up and grinned. He was no longer in the trees but in a field of thick grass.

"Bear, you did it. You're the best," said Bob, standing up and hugging him. "Now, you go back to Mrs Remus now. Go on, boy."

Bear walked back into the woods and was soon out of sight. Then Bob set off. He was glad to be out of the woods but aware that he still had two fields to cross and a whole festival to search before he would be back with his family.

Bob hadn't gone far when he heard movement behind him. He turned. It was just sheep, four of them. Fine. Sheep were harmless. Not like lions. He began walking again – but so did the sheep. Bob looked at them. They stopped and looked at him.

"Could you go away?" Bob asked.

The sheep only stared at him. He walked; they followed.

"Look, what do you want?" Bob shouted, irritated now. "Food? Is it food?"

Bob found the onion in his bag and threw it. The sheep ran over to it. Relieved, Bob set off again, but when he glanced behind, he was shocked to see that two sheep were still following him. One had a scar on its nose, and the other had a chunk missing from its ear in the shape of a bite.

Bob grabbed the cream cake from his bag and threw that, but the two sheep stepped on it, crushing it into the grass, and kept coming towards him.

He sped up, keen to get away from these stalker sheep, but when he checked again, they were even nearer. Holy crackers! Were they on wheels to make them faster? Or wearing little sheep jet packs?

Bob broke into a jog, swishing fast through the tall grass until he made it to the stream

that divided the two fields. He glanced quickly left and right. No bridge! Oh great! He had two stalker sheep on his tail and needed to get across the stream and ...

THUMP.

Something nudged Bob and he jolted forwards, towards the rushing water. Then another nudge. The sheep were shoving him with their hard black noses.

"Stop it! Get off me!" Bob squealed. "You're going to push me in and I can't—"

The last word of Bob's sentence – "swim" – was lost as he hit the water. He thrashed wildly, gasping and gulping until he realised he could feel the bottom with his hands as well as his feet. Bob stood up. The water only reached his knees.

"Oh, thank goodness," Bob muttered. He waded towards the opposite bank and pulled himself out. Dripping wet and shaking, he looked back at the sheep.

"You!" Bob yelled, waving his fist. "You two are *pigs*! You're horrible. The most horrible sheep I've ever met. Stay there, OK?"

Then he turned and ...

"Geese!" Bob gasped, freezing on the spot.

There were lots of them, staring at Bob with their pale blue eyes. He edged forwards, but the geese flapped their big white wings and tried to peck his trainers. Not again! Another animal obstacle! Another farmyard foe!

What else did he have in his bag that might help? Bob reached in and found the washing-up liquid. Perfect! He flipped off the lid, took aim and squeezed. A jet of foamy liquid shot out, making the geese scatter. Some geese snapped at the bubbles that were now flying in the air,

and others ran around honking and skidding on
the slippery grass.

Now's my chance to get past, Bob thought,
and he charged towards them. He felt wings
beat against his legs and saw feathers flying,
but he didn't stop. Bob had almost made

it through the geese when a single goose appeared right in front of him, its yellow beak open. *It's going to peck my nose off*, Bob thought. *It's going to poke my eyes out!*

Bob's hand went to his pocket and he found the old chewing gum stashed there, now soft and warm. He lobbed the gum towards the goose, shouting, "Here, catch!" Bob watched as the huge bird's beak closed on the grey squishy lump – and got stuck shut.

"Yes!" Bob yelled, racing away. He could see the gate up ahead – he was nearly there, but hold on, what now? Cows were trotting towards him! Where had they come from? Bob braced himself. No turning back now. He had come this far. He was ready.

Again he reached into his bag. He found the saucepan and threw it, scaring one of the cows into running off. Next, he threw the two teaspoons, which hit one cow on the ear and one on the nose, stopping them.

"Bingo!" Bob roared. "You've been teaspooned! Now for the rest of you."

Bob threw the bean tin, but the remaining cows ignored it. He tried chucking the teabags, which did nothing. Bob realised, as he scrabbled in his bag, that there was only string and paper clips left. All useless. Then he felt the party blower. His last and only hope. Bob raised it to his lips and blew hard.

PARMP!

The last few cows stopped suddenly. Bob blew again as he ran nearer – *PARMP*, *PARMP*, *PARMP*. They didn't move. He *PARMPED* again, getting closer, and then the cows suddenly scattered and skipped away, scared by a red-foil party blower. Finally, Bob's path was clear. He dashed forwards, vaulted over the gate with a *WHOOP!* and landed in a heap on the other side.

CHAPTER 8

Bob Takes to the Stage

Bob looked up to see a man in cord trousers and a checked shirt.

"Why on earth were you blowing a trumpet at my cows?" the man asked, frowning with confusion.

"Sorry, I didn't know what else to do," Bob panted, struggling to his feet. "I've been attacked by sheep and geese and now cows, and, and ..."

"All right, son, take a breath," the man said. "Looks like you've been through the wars."

Bob glanced down at himself. His clothes were wet and streaked with goose poo, and Cosmo's trainers were covered in grass stains.

"Are you ill?" the man asked. "You're awfully green."

"It's camouflage," Bob said. "I'm on a mission to find my family. I'm looking for the Green Yon Gathering at Old Munty's Farm. Am I close?"

"Close? You're here, lad. I'm Farmer Munty."

"Really? So I've made it?" Bob said, smiling. "I can't believe it!"

"Congratulations," said Farmer Munty. "Now, if you want to find your folks, your best bet is to travel on Mabel."

Bob wondered if Mabel was a cool electric scooter or a speedy tractor. But Farmer Munty led him over to a stable and inside was a stocky grey donkey.

"Vehicles aren't allowed on the festival site," Farmer Munty explained. "But Mabel here will be faster than walking."

"But I've never ridden a donkey before," Bob said, shocked.

"Nothing to it!" said Farmer Munty, helping Bob onto Mabel's back. "Just hold on."

Bob grabbed the reins tight as Mabel trotted out of the farmyard. Then he heard it – the noise of the festival. Music, drums, singing, laughing. Bob followed the sound, turned a corner and, finally, there it was: the Green Yon Gathering.

Bob had a good view from up on Mabel's back. There were thousands of people – a sea of bodies spreading into the distance. The whole town and more were here, all having fun. To his left there was Worm Charming, to his right he could see Jump the Goat. Up ahead, some kids were playing Spin the Cowpat. There were two men demonstrating how to make socks from moss, a chicken orchestra and a stall selling Buttered Rogers – traditional buns that smelled of plums and honey.

It all looked brilliant. Bob wanted to join in,
to try his hand at Toss the Turnip and Woodlouse
Rolling, but he couldn't stop. Operation Find My
Family was still on. He urged Mabel forwards.

In the distance, Bob spotted someone
juggling what looked like frying pans. River?
No, that wasn't him. He noticed people gathered

around a woman reading poetry – was it his mum? But when she looked up, Bob saw it wasn't her. Then he heard banjos on the main stage and rode nearer, but there was no sign of his dad anywhere.

"This is hopeless," said Bob, with a sigh that made Mabel's ears twitch. "How will I ever find my family in this crowd?"

Then an announcement boomed out: "Ladies and gentlemen, please raise your eyes to the skies for … the Moth Arrows."

Bob gasped. He'd always wanted to see this legendary moth aerobatics display team. Here they were, flying in tight formation, shaped like a diamond, then an exclamation mark, then a pineapple. They swooped low over the crowd and everyone "oohed" and "ahhed". Everyone except Mabel, who flicked her tail and kicked her back legs.

"Easy there," said Bob. "It's only moths."

Mabel continued to fidget as the Moth Arrows spun around. They flew back towards the crowd and swooped over her head. Mabel let out a panicked "Eee-aww!" and bolted.

"Eeek! Mabel, what are you doing? Oof!" Bob said as he bounced around on her back.

People screamed and dived clear as Mabel bombed towards the main stage. Then, with a giant leap, she jumped right onto it, scattering banjo players like skittles. Bob was amazed to find himself still on Mabel's back, but for how much longer?

The moths were still fluttering above, making Mabel rear up like a wild stallion in a rodeo. The crowd pressed forwards to watch as Mabel kicked and bucked, flicking her head, swishing her tail and eee-awwing loudly.

All Bob could do was hang on. He was bounced and jolted until, eventually, Mabel grew

tired. After one final buck, she stood still in the
centre of the stage, panting.

Shaking, Bob slipped off her sweaty back and
stared blankly at the audience. Why were they

clapping? Why had the Moth Arrows written AWESOME! in fluttering letters above? For him? For not falling off Mabel? He bowed slightly, and everyone cheered wildly. *This is new*, Bob thought.

Then he spotted two people pushing through the crowd.

"Mum! Dad! Up here!" Bob yelled to them, waving.

"We're coming!" they shouted. His parents climbed onto the stage and squashed Bob into a giant hug. The crowd roared even more.

"I've found you at last," Bob said. He breathed in their familiar Mum and Dad smell, feeling relief wash over him.

"We're so sorry we left you behind," Mum said. "It was a terrible mistake. As soon as I realised you weren't here, I contacted Sergeant Bill. Did he tell you?"

"Nobody told me anything," said Bob. "I had to work it out alone. I saw a poster for the festival and guessed you'd be here. Then I got lost in the woods and rode a dog and was attacked by stalker sheep and nasty geese. I even had to teaspoon some cows. It was wild!"

"But you made it! You're so brave. And so green," said his dad, touching Bob's camouflaged cheeks.

"I had no money," Bob went on. "I survived on cream cakes and tinned peaches, but I had to find you."

More people were climbing onto the stage now – Bob's brothers and sisters.

"Nice work, Bob," River shouted.

"Amazing rodeo skills," said Cosmo. "Cool trainers too. It's OK. You can keep them."

"I couldn't take my eyes off you, Bob," Arwen said.

"You're a performer like us after all," said India.

Farmer Munty appeared too. "And you're a donkey-whisperer," he said to Bob. "No one's ever been able to stay on Mabel when she's been spooked by moths, but you just did."

Then Farmer Munty shouted into the microphone: "Give it up for Bob!"

The crowd cheered again. Bob waved, trying to soak it all in. He spotted Mrs Remus and Bear – they were here too! They waved back, and Bill Junior and Sergeant Bill were clapping. Bob beamed with joy and then felt his feet come off the ground – River and Cosmo lifted him onto their shoulders and bounced him around. Bob's shrieks and laughter were drowned out by Farmer Munty on the microphone.

"Now, there's only one way to follow that," shouted the farmer. "The Ceremony of the Burning of the Rugs! Please make your way to the Upper Field – it's about to start."

The crowd gave another huge roar and then everyone set off.

"Shall we go and burn some rugs together?" Dad called up to Bob.

"Together," said Bob.

"TOGETHER!" Bob's whole family shouted – well, Arwen opera-wailed it.

With Bob still high on his brothers' shoulders, they ran off the stage and towards the bonfire, which was blazing brightly in the distance.

CHAPTER 9

Last Words

Bob's Abandonment Journal

Final entry

*Reader, I survived. I refused to perish
alone here in my bedroom. I faced
danger and despair – and overcame it all!*

*Mum and Dad are still apologising
for leaving me behind, which I'm quite
enjoying. But Mum says I can't adopt*

Mabel and keep her in the garden. We'll see about that.

River, Cosmo, Arwen and India are noticing me at last. They say I am an adventurer, like Lofty Gills, and an amazing bare-back donkey rider who made a crowd of thousands cheer. True.

I have stuck some old chewing gum under my desk again, just in case. And I never leave home without a party blower now. Be prepared. And be brave. That's what I've learned. It's the Bob Bunyon way.

Over and out.

Our books are tested
for children and young people by
children and young people.

Thanks to everyone who consulted on
a manuscript for their time and effort in
helping us to make our books better
for our readers.